Sam and Jack
Three Stories

Alex Moran
Illustrated by Tim Bowers

Green Light Readers
Harcourt, Inc.
Orlando   Austin   New York   San Diego   London

A Surprise

I see a mat.

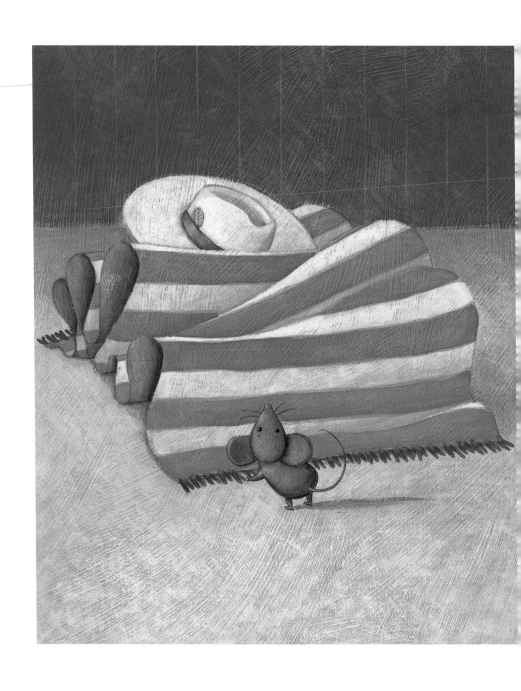

I see a hat on a mat.

I see a tail on a mat.

I see a cat on a mat.

It is Jack the cat!

Jack

Are you a cat?

I am a cat.

Are you a friend?

I am a friend.

I am your funny friend, Jack.

Sam

I am Sam.

I am little.

I am big.

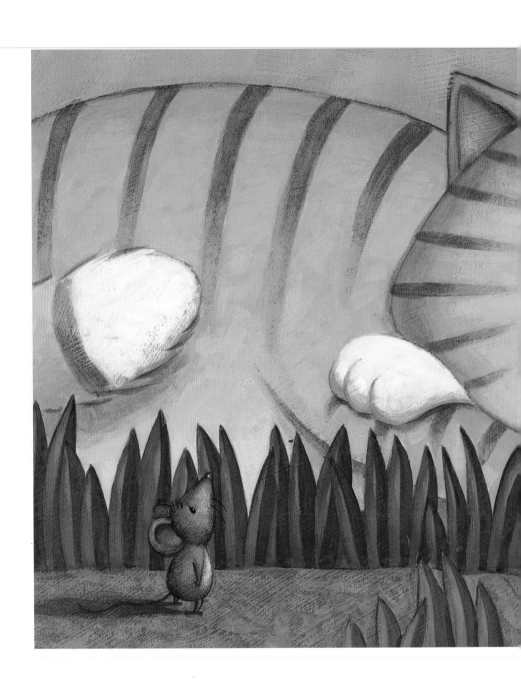

I am sad.

I am happy.

Make a Friend

It's fun to make a new friend!

WHAT YOU'LL NEED

 paper plate

 yarn

 crayons or markers

 Popsicle sticks

 pasta

 tape

1 Make a paper plate puppet that looks like your new friend.

2 Have your friend make a puppet that looks like you.

3 When you're done, tape a Popsicle stick to the back of each puppet.

Then you can:

- Let your puppets do the talking.
  Use the puppets to tell stories about you and your new friend.

- Have a puppet show.
  Act out a way to be a good friend.

Meet the Illustrator

Tim Bowers loves to draw pictures of animals. Dogs were his favorite animals to paint when he was a young boy. He painted many pictures of his own dog, which still hang in his parents' house today! Now he enjoys drawing all sorts of different animals, like Jack the cat and Sam the mouse in this story.

Requests for permission to make copies of any part of the work should be submitted online at www.harcourt.com/contact or mailed to the following address: Permissions Department, Houghton Miffflin Harcourt Publishing Company, 6277 Sea Harbor Drive, Orlando, Florida 32887-6777.

www.HarcourtBooks.com

First Green Light Readers edition 2001
Green Light Readers is a trademark of Harcourt, Inc., registered in the United States of America and/or other jurisdictions.

The Library of Congress has cataloged an earlier edition as follows:
Moran, Alex.
Sam and Jack/Alex Moran; illustrated by Tim Bowers.
p. cm.
"Green Light Readers."
Summary: Sam the mouse and Jack the cat
overcome their differences and become friends.
[1. Cats—Fiction. 2. Mice—Fiction. 3. Friendship—Fiction.]
I. Bowers, Tim, ill. II. Title.
PZ7.M788193Sam 2001
[E]—dc21 2001000413
ISBN 978-0-15-204822-8
ISBN 978-0-15-204862-4 (pb)

A C E G H F D B
E G I J H F D (pb)

Ages 4-6
Grade: K-1
Guided Reading Level: C
Reading Recovery Level: 4

Green Light Readers
For the reader who's ready to GO!

"A must-have for any family with a beginning reader."—*Boston Sunday Herald*

"You can't go wrong with adding several copies of these terrific books to your beginning-to-read collection."—*School Library Journal*

"A winner for the beginner."—*Booklist*

Five Tips to Help Your Child Become a Great Reader

1. Get involved. Reading aloud to and with your child is just as important as encouraging your child to read independently.

2. Be curious. Ask questions about what your child is reading.

3. Make reading fun. Allow your child to pick books on subjects that interest her or him.

4. Words are everywhere—not just in books. Practice reading signs, packages, and cereal boxes with your child.

5. Set a good example. Make sure your child sees YOU reading.

Why Green Light Readers Is the Best Series for Your New Reader

- Created exclusively for beginning readers by some of the biggest and brightest names in children's books

- Reinforces the reading skills your child is learning in school

- Encourages children to read—and finish—books by themselves

- Offers extra enrichment through fun, age-appropriate activities unique to each story

- Incorporates characteristics of the Reading Recovery program used by educators

- Developed with Harcourt School Publishers and credentialed educational consultants